THE STRANGE BLUE CREATURE

PAUL BOROVSKY

Hyperion Books for Children
New York

For my Dad and Vera

For information address Hyperion Books for Children,
114 Fifth Avenue, New York, New York 10011.

FIRST EDITION
1   3   5   7   9   10   8   6   4   2

Library of Congress Cataloging-in-Publication Data

Borovsky, Paul.
The strange blue creature / Paul Borovsky—1st ed.   p.   cm.
Summary: A strange blue creature threatens to eat all the crayons
in a tiny kingdom, until the princess shows him how they are used.
ISBN 1-56282-434-1—ISBN 1-56282-435-X (lib. bdg.)
[1. Crayons—Fiction.   2. Princesses—Fiction.   3. Artists—Fiction.]   I. Title.
PZ7.B64849St   1993   [E]—dc20
92-54864   CIP   AC

The artwork for each picture is prepared using pen and ink and gouache.
This book is set in 18-point Syntax.

VROOM

SWOOSH

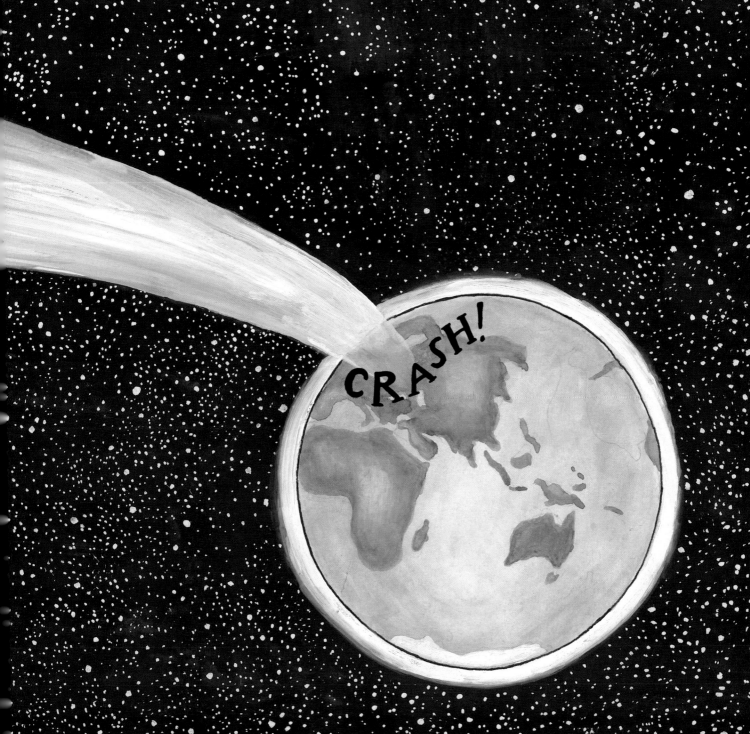

When the smoke cleared away, a strange blue creature appeared.

The creature stomped his foot. "I'm HUNGRY!" he roared. Looking around, he spied a castle on top of a hill.

The blue creature peered through a window and saw a princess sharpening her crayons.

"Red, yellow, green, orange, purple," said the princess.
"All ready to be put back in their box."

With a crash, the strange blue creature leapt through the window and gobbled up all the crayons.

"How dare you eat my crayons!" cried the princess. "I try so hard to keep them neat and tidy in my crayon box, and now you come and eat them all up!"

But the strange blue creature just smiled, licked his lips, and jumped out the window.

Down the road he saw a school yard filled with children.

The creature raced into their classrooms to look through the desks and gobbled up every crayon he could find. Even the broken ones.

He ate the dust from the crayon sharpeners for dessert.

"Something must be done about this horrible creature!
He's eating all the crayons!" moaned the princess.

So she sent her soldiers after the creature immediately.

The soldiers marched toward the creature. But the strange blue creature made such a scary face that they all ran away.

He then broke into all the stores in the kingdom, devouring all the crayons he could find.

"That's enough!" exclaimed the princess. "I'll have to do something about this myself." She set off to confront the strange blue creature, who had just discovered the crayon factory.

"You strange, blue, *greedy* creature!" said the princess.
"Don't you know what crayons are for?"

Not waiting for a reply, the princess picked up her favorite colors. Since there was no paper around, she started to draw pictures on the crayon factory wall.

"You see: Blue is the color of the sea. So if you want to be at the seaside, you use the blue crayon. Orange is the color of fish swimming in the sea. Yellow is the color of the shining sun. And then there are green islands and purple birds and people and boats and…"

The strange blue creature was very curious. He picked up a crayon. He drew a line and then a circle. He tried another color, and then another. He started to draw. He drew and drew and drew…

…and drew straight on into the night. Meanwhile, the princess and all the people in the kingdom slept peacefully. They knew their crayons were safe because the strange blue creature was still drawing.

When everyone woke up and looked outside, they knew it was the end of the strange blue creature…

…and the beginning of the greatest artist the town would ever know.